SCIENCE COURT

TO SERVE AND OBSERVE™

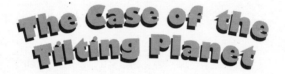

The Case of the Tilting Planet

Adapted by Craig Strasshofer

Based on an orginal TV episode written and created by Tom Snyder, Bill Braudis, and David Dockterman

Illustrated by Bob Thibeault and Kristine Koob

Troll

HEATHER AND THE WEATHER

Heather Hancock had been looking forward to her Australian vacation. She'd saved pennies in her piggy bank, collected bottles and cans for recycling, and done extra odd jobs in order to raise the money to pay for the trip.

Finally here she was, all by herself in the middle of the Australian outback. In her pith helmet and sunglasses, she was prepared for the blistering heat of an Australian summer. Her camera hung from her neck, ready to capture dazzling images of mirages, oases, and the sun blazing down on the parched, sandy landscape.

Yet, even though it was June, it was not hot. So there stood Heather. She was alone. She was cold. And she was very, very mad. Yes, Heather was mad about the weather.

"What kind of summer vacation is this?" she asked herself, since there was nobody else around. "I fly all the way to Australia, in June, and the temperature hasn't been above fifty degrees Fahrenheit. Here I am in the land down under, the land of billabongs and sheep and shrimp on the barbie, the land of . . ."

As she stood in the outback, shivering and muttering to herself, Heather heard a low rumbling sound. It seemed to be coming from a fast-moving whirlwind of desert dust headed straight toward her.

"The land of . . . kangaroos!" Heather screamed. She took off running with a large and probably dangerous kangaroo hopping behind her in hot pursuit. Heather ran all the way back to the airport and took the next plane home.

2

SHOWDOWN WITH SHEP

Heather cut short her dream vacation partly because of the kangaroos, but mostly because of the cold. When she returned home, she went to the library to find out why it was so cold in Australia during the month of June. Her research led her to a startling revelation—the earth was moving *away* from the sun.

"Oh no," she said. "The same thing is going to happen here at home that happened in Australia. We're not going to have any summer."

She was disappointed, of course, but not for the obvious reason. She had been looking forward to taking a synchronized swimming class for which she had signed up and paid before she left on her trip. Who would want to go swimming when it was only fifty degrees Fahrenheit? "I've been tricked," she said. "I'm going to get my money back."

First thing the next morning she was standing outside Shep Sherman's office. The sign above the door read:

Shep Sherman's Learning Center

Learn Synchronized Swimming this Summer in My New Outdoor Pool! Make a Big Splash at Parties!

"Harrumph," Heather harrumphed with a frown. "There isn't even going to *be* a summer. I'm going to give Shep Sherman a piece of my mind."

She marched in and plopped herself down in a chair in front of Shep's desk. She glared at Shep and then at the sign on the wall behind him that listed all the things he claimed he could teach.

At Shep Sherman's Learning Center
You Can Learn How to:
Play Chess
Shoe Horses
Cook Creole
Fix Lawn Mowers
Speak Pig Latin
Build Soapbox Derby Cars
Clean Fish
Play the Accordion
Ride a Bike
Synchronize Swim

Other than the sign and the desk, there wasn't much in Shep's tiny office besides a bookshelf lined with every how-to book you could imagine.

Shep was a friendly fellow, and he liked to think of himself as being a good teacher, although he didn't really know all that much about playing chess, shoeing horses, cooking Creole, or fixing lawn mowers.

"Good morning. Heather Hancock, isn't it? It's very nice to see you," he said with a smile. "How can I help you?"

"How dare you!" Heather shot back.

"I beg your pardon?" asked Shep.

"Don't play dumb with me," Heather growled. "Because two can play at that game. And I'll even play alone if I have to."

"I don't know what you're talking about, Ms. Hancock," Shep replied as politely as he could. He didn't understand how Heather could play dumb all by herself, but he thought it might make a good class: *How to Play Dumb All by Yourself.*

"You know there's not going to be a summer this year, don't you?" Heather said accusingly.

"What?" Shep couldn't believe what he was hearing.

Heather held up a book entitled *The Earth's Orbit.* "I've done a little reading," she said, "and I've found out that the earth is moving away from the sun."

"It is?" Shep asked.

"It is," Heather said firmly. "That's why when I was in Australia it was only fifty degrees Fahrenheit."

"I didn't sneeze," said Shep.

"Not gesundheit, Fahrenheit," Heather corrected Shep. "It was June, but it didn't feel like June. People were even calling it winter."

"Well, that's their business," Shep said.

"But I've heard Australia is a very beautiful place."

"It is," Heather agreed. "The Great Barrier Reef was incredible. But that's not the point. The point is, I've stumbled onto your plan. You're charging people for swimming lessons in your outdoor pool this summer, but you've known all along there isn't going to be a summer."

"This is crazy!" Shep exclaimed. He was looking forward to enjoying his new outdoor pool just as much as anybody else.

"But it all makes perfect sense," Heather replied. "You won't have to teach anybody anything. It will be too cold for swimming. You'll just sit back and count your money."

Shep decided to try a little humor to relieve the tension. "Actually," he said with a smile, "I count on an accountant to count my money."

Heather did not think that was funny.

She just kept scowling at him.

"But even so," Shep went on, "I can't give you back all the money you paid for your synchronized swimming lessons because I don't have it all. If you want to wait . . ."

"I'm going to take you to Science Court, Shep Sherman," Heather declared. "And I'm going to prove that summer's not coming and that you knew about it all along."

Shep was totally bewildered now. "You know," he said, "you're really giving me too much credit here. . . . I don't really know that much about what causes the seasons, and I—"

But Heather wouldn't let him finish. "And," she ranted, "I'm also going to tell the entire world not to take your synchronized swimming classes."

"The entire world?" Shep asked nervously. "Aren't you overreacting just a . . . just a . . . just a whole bunch?"

"Mr. Sherman," Heather said, rising from her chair, "I may be a fool, and I may be stupid, and I may be forgetful . . . but I'm not a fool. And when a cause is worth fighting for, I fight to the finish."

With that she turned on her heel, lost her balance from trying to turn on her heel, regained her balance, and stormed out, slamming the door behind her.

Shep sat there for a moment scratching his head, although it didn't really itch. "I don't know what she's talking about," he said to himself, since he was the only one there. "But whatever it is, it sure sounds like big trouble."

3

SAVAGE TO THE RESCUE

Heather may have been a fool, and she may have been stupid, and she may have been forgetful, but she was also a person of action. She had the name of a top-notch Science Court attorney—Doug Savage, Legend in His Own Mind. She'd gotten Doug's name from a coupon Doug had attached to her windshield when she parked at the local supermarket. She wasted no time in setting up an appointment with Doug, who agreed to meet with her at his home.

When Heather got to Doug's place, she

knocked on the door several times without receiving a response. Yet she was sure she could hear movement inside. She opened the door, stepped in, and saw a man with a wild shock of hair. He was balanced precariously on a ladder with a couple of rungs missing, hanging empty picture frames on the wall.

"Mr. Savage?" she asked.

"Yes, that's me," the man on the ladder replied smugly. "Doug Savage, Science Court attorney extraordinaire. You must be Heather Hancock. I've been expecting you."

"If you don't mind my asking," Heather said, "what are you doing?"

"Just a little decorating. I like to think of my home as something of a showplace."

"But the frames are empty," Heather pointed out.

"Well, sure," Doug said. "The frames are empty now, but someday I hope to put all kinds of awards and certificates in them. This frame is going to be for the 'Science Court Attorney of the Year Award.'"

"Wow," said Heather, trying to think of something positive to say. "It looks like you're halfway there."

"Thanks," Doug replied cheerfully. Just then he hit his thumb with the hammer, but he tried hard not to show how much it hurt. "Uh, ouch and stuff," he mumbled, sucking his thumb and hoping Heather wouldn't notice. "Now, what was that ridiculous story you were telling me over the phone?"

"Ridiculous? . . . Well, perhaps," she said. "But when I was in Australia it never got above fifty degrees Fahrenheit."

"I didn't sneeze," said Doug.

"What?" Heather hesitated. "No, not gesundheit, Fahrenheit. It didn't get above fifty degrees Fahrenheit, and it was June."

"That does seem odd," Doug said as he swung his hammer again, missing the nail and knocking a large hole in the wall. "But maybe it was just lousy weather."

"No," Heather explained. "I did a little research, and I found out that the earth is moving away from the sun."

"What? It can't do that. Can it?" Doug asked.

"Yes, it can," Heather replied. "And it is."

Doug was on the verge of panic now. "Where will we hide? What will we eat? How will we get a tan? What will we have to do? Move?"

"That's not going to do any good," Heather told him.

"Well, did you notify the National Weather Bureau?" Doug asked.

"No," said Heather.

"The White House?"

"I haven't gotten around to it."

"NASA?"

"What good would it do to call the

Bahamas?" Heather wondered, with a hint of irritation in her voice.

"No, not Nassau. NASA—the Nautical Astronauts Service Association," Doug told her as he dropped a picture frame, the glass shattering on the floor.

"Oh, them. I tried. They won't take my calls anymore," said Heather.

Doug tried to pound in a nail as he took a moment to think about what Heather had said. This time the nail bent, gouging another hole in the wall.

"Well, what exactly does it mean that the earth is moving away from the sun?" Doug asked.

"It means that it's not going to be as hot, which means no summer at all. It has already happened in Australia, and now it's going to happen here," Heather answered.

"That's incredible, absolutely incredible. The people need to be warned. They need to cancel their vacation plans before it's too late," Doug concluded. "But what does Shep Sherman have to do with all of this? Surely it's not his fault."

"Please don't call me Shirley," Heather said. "My name is Heather. And the reason I want to sue Shep Sherman is that I have already paid for fifty of his synchronized swimming lessons because water ballet has always been my secret passion."

"Oh, I get it." Doug nodded, almost losing his balance. "Since there's not going to be a summer, Shep will never have to teach the classes, so he makes all that money for doing nothing."

"That's right," said Heather. "It's a scam. Shep knows there isn't going to be a summer. And I know he knows. And he knows I know he knows. And now you know I know Shep knows I know he knows."

"I'm getting dizzy," said Doug.

"And Shep won't give me my money back, either. He told me I'd have to wait," Heather complained.

"Well," Doug declared with lawyer-like confidence, "I think a little visit to Science Court will get you your money back and teach Shep Sherman a lesson. You can count on me . . ."

Just then Doug stepped on the part of the ladder that said THIS IS NOT A STEP and went tumbling to the floor.

"*Waaa,*" he cried on the way down.

Heather stayed just long enough to make sure Doug was not seriously injured. On her way home, she couldn't help wondering if she'd chosen the right attorney for the job.

4

SHEP AND THE DREAM TEAM

That same day, in another part of town, Shep Sherman was sitting in the casually elegant office of Science Court attorney Alison Krempel and her assistant, Tim. Alison was a dedicated lawyer with a love for science. Tim was Alison's trustworthy assistant, a law student at the city college who was eager to learn. In fact, Tim was eager to help Alison in any way he could. The three of them were reviewing some legal documents Shep had brought along.

"This is pretty wild," Alison said,

glancing up from the pile of papers on her desk.

"Well, actually, Ms. Krempel," Shep told her with pride, "synchronized swimming, or water ballet, is a legitimate Olympic event and very beautiful."

"I'm talking about Heather Hancock's accusation," Alison explained as she flipped through the papers in the folder once again.

"Oh," Shep replied. "Yeah, that is wild. But she's got a good point. I mean, if the earth really *is* moving away from the sun, we're in trouble."

"Shep, don't worry," said Alison calmly. "There is going to be a summer. It's clear from these documents that Heather Hancock has blown some facts out of proportion and jumped to a totally wrong conclusion, that's all."

"Actually, that's what I like about her," said Shep. "She's imaginative."

Shep Sherman was the kind of person who liked everybody. That's what made him a good teacher, even when he didn't quite know what he was talking about.

"Why didn't you just give Heather Hancock her money back if she didn't want to take the swimming classes?" Tim asked.

"I was going to," Shep said with a shrug. "I just couldn't do it right away. The next thing I knew, she was accusing me of running a scam."

"Well," Alison said, closing the folder with an air of authority, "I think we can prove that there will be a summer and that your classes are legitimate."

Shep sighed with relief, but then he frowned. "You know," he said glumly, "Ms. Hancock wants to get me banned from teaching, period. And I love to teach. I live to teach. And forgive me for blowing my own horn, but I'm good at it."

". . . What about that cooking class you taught that made everybody sick?" Tim asked hesitantly.

"Well, that one . . ." said Shep. "The problem then was that I didn't really know what I was doing. But anybody who got sick got his or her money back. Plus," he added, "I paid for everybody's dry cleaning."

Alison didn't like to hear negative things about her clients. She was a firm believer in positive thinking. "Yes, well, uh . . ." she said.

Alison was a good lawyer, and to be a good lawyer you have to understand people. Just as she had anticipated, her meaningless mumbling had its effect on Shep Sherman. "So . . . anyway, the point is, Ms. Krempel, will you and Tim help me?" he asked.

"Mr. Sherman," Alison replied, "we'd be glad to help you."

Alison was happy to take a case she thought she could win. She was happy to fight for the underdog. She was happy that she had such a deep knowledge of human behavior. And she was happy that she would be taking her summer vacation as soon as the trial was over.

Tim was happy to be involved in a case he could really sink his teeth into. He was happy to study around the clock to learn everything he had to know to help win the case. And he was happy just to be near Alison as much as he possibly could.

Shep was happy to have found a lawyer who inspired confidence the way Alison Krempel did. He was happy to think he might be able to win the case. And he was happy that even if he lost the case, he would always know in his heart he was a good teacher, even when he didn't know what he was talking about.

5

THE TRIAL BEGINS

The day of the big trial finally arrived. It wasn't long before everyone was assembled in the courtroom. Heather Hancock sat at one table with her attorney, Doug Savage. Across the aisle, Alison and Tim sat with their client, the defendant, Shep Sherman. Stenographer Fred was at his desk, his nimble fingers poised. It was stenographer Fred's job to record everything that everybody said during a Science Court trial.

In the front row of spectators, right behind Doug Savage, sat a girl named

Micaela. She loved Science Court and never missed a session. In fact, sometimes it seemed as if she knew more about what was going on than anyone else did—especially Doug.

Jen Betters positioned herself in front of the camera, waited for her cue, and then began her broadcast. "Hi. I'm Jen Betters reporting from Science Court, where science is the law and scientific thinking rules. Today we have the case of the lost summer. Oh, here comes Judge Stone now."

WHAT'S A DEFENDANT?

THAT'S YOU, A PERSON WHO IS BEING ACCUSED OF A CRIME OR BEING SUED FOR DAMAGES.

"All rise," said Fred.

All the participants rose, then took their seats again as Judge Stone quickly reviewed the papers on her bench. "Okay," she began. "Let me get this straight. Heather Hancock charges that Shep Sherman knows there's not going to be a summer this year. Is that right, Mr. Savage?"

The jury murmured with anxiety at the very thought of there being no summer.

"That's right," Doug replied. "But Shep continues to collect payments from people for swimming lessons that he has no intention of teaching."

"It's not just swimming," Shep broke in. "It's synchronized swimming. You know, water ballet? It's really very beautiful."

"No kidding?" said Judge Stone. "I've always wanted to do that."

"Well, you can sign up," said Shep.

"Objection," Doug shouted.

"We'll talk later," Judge Stone whispered to Shep.

"Your Honor," Doug continued, "I don't know why you're wasting your time. There's not going to be a summer this year."

This time he spoke with such certainty that some members of the jury began to cry. Doug knew he had them right in the palm of his hand, which made the palm of his hand very sweaty, but it was what he wanted. He continued to play upon their emotions. "Maybe," he said soothingly, "there will be one next year, if the earth moves back toward the sun."

"You know," Judge Stone remarked, "I did hear that there was cooler weather in the forecast, but—"

"And that's only the beginning, Your Honor," Doug interrupted. "That's why we want Shep to give back all the money he's made from these so-called swimming classes, as well as agree to never teach another class again—ever!"

"Okay, Mr. Savage," said Judge Stone.

"Ever," Doug repeated.

"Thank you," Judge Stone said firmly. "Ms. Krempel, your opening statement, please."

"Thank you very much, Your Honor," Alison began. "Good people of the jury . . ."

"I always forget to call them 'good people,'" Doug whispered to Heather. "She has a nice way with words."

"Summer is coming," Alison went on. "Shep's synchronized swimming classes are legitimate. He's an excellent teacher. There's no scam, and there's no bizarre climate change. This whole thing is just a bunch of gobbledygook. We will prove that summer will come—rain or shine."

"Or snow?" Doug mocked.

"Mr. Savage," Judge Stone said, "got a witness?"

"Yes, I do, Your Honor," Doug replied. "And I might add she's 'out of this world.'" Doug laughed, but everyone else in the court-room remained silent and stonefaced. So Doug continued, "I call Dr. Julie Bean to the stand."

Dr. Julie Bean had bright blue eyes and a peculiar hair style that made her look like an elf. She was an expert on all things scientific, although today she was appearing in court as an orbit expert, which is really hard to say three times fast.

"Orbit expert, orbit expert, orbit expert," said Doug.

"Orbit expert, orbit expert, orbit expert," said Alison.

"Orbit expert, orbit expert, orbit expert," said Micaela.

"Orbit expert, orbit expert, orbit expert," said Judge Stone. "That's tough."

"Can I try it once?" Fred asked.

"No, that's okay," said Judge Stone. "Go ahead, Mr. Savage."

"Dr. Bean," Doug began, "the earth travels in an orbit around the sun, does it not?"

"Yes, it does," Julie replied.

"Now, can you please tell me, I mean, this courtroom, exactly what an orbit is?" Doug asked.

"Sure," Julie said agreeably. "An orbit is a curved path that a planet, for example, makes around the sun."

"You mean, like the earth?" Doug asked.

"Yes," Julie responded. "It's also what the moon does around the earth. Like this . . ." She pulled out a demonstration model with a miniature sun and planets that moved. She tilted the earth slightly, then showed how it revolves around the sun. "See?" she said.

"Be careful," Doug warned her. "You're tilting the earth. We wouldn't want anyone falling off now, would we?" He laughed and laughed. Nobody else did, though.

MY HEAD IS WHIRLING. STOP THE WORLD. I WANT TO GET OFF!

"No one would fall off," Julie assured him. "The earth has a lot of gravity to keep everything on it. Gravity is the same force that holds the earth in its orbit."

"I knew that," Doug said defensively.

"And besides," Julie added, "the earth really is tilted as it revolves around the sun . . . like this." She demonstrated the way the earth is tilted on its axis.

Doug turned to Heather and whispered, "I just want you to know I'm saying this next dumb thing on purpose."

"Wow," said Heather. "I didn't know you said them on purpose."

"Sometimes," Doug replied. Then he turned back to Julie and asked, "So, the earth goes around the sun in a big circle, right?"

"Well, actually, it's not quite a circle," Julie responded.

"Oh, really?" Doug said slyly. "It's not a circle?"

"No. It's more of an oval shape, like this." Julie produced a chart showing the earth's orbit around the sun. "We call this a slightly elliptical orbit."

"Wait a minute," Stenographer Fred piped up. "I missed that."

"Read my lips, Fred," said Judge Stone. "Slight-ly el-lip-ti-cal."

"Could you say that again?" Fred asked.

"Did you read my lips?" asked Judge Stone.

"Yes," Fred replied, "but I lost my place."

"Slightly elliptical," the judge repeated.

"Okay, I got it," said Fred. "Slightly elliptical."

"Okay, then." Doug continued with his questioning. "So, sometimes the earth is closer to the sun as it revolves in its 365-day trip around the sun, right?"

"That's a whole year!" Fred exclaimed.

"Yes," said Julie, rolling her eyes. "You're both right."

A troubled murmur arose from the jury box—365 days in a year, that was important testimony.

Doug turned to Heather and said, "This witness is like putty in my hands . . . but that's good."

"For example," Julie continued, drawing attention back to her chart, "at this point here, the earth is about five million kilometers farther away from the sun than it is at this point here."

"Five million kilometers, that's a huge distance . . ." said Doug.

"Well, not really . . ." Julie responded.

"Isn't that equal to about . . ." Doug whipped out a calculator and calculated wildly. "Uh . . . three miles?"

"Three miles?" Julie asked, puzzled.

"Oh, wait a minute." Doug calculated some more. "I mean . . . three million miles?" he said somewhat uncertainly.

"Yeah, that's about right," Julie agreed.

"*Yesss,*" said Doug, giving himself the thumbs-up sign. "Now, that's a huge distance."

"Well, yeah," Julie replied, "but . . ."

"Dr. Bean," Doug persisted, "could you walk to my house if I lived five million kilometers away?"

"No," said Julie.

"Can you ride your bike five million kilometers?" Doug asked.

"No," Julie answered.

"Of course not," said Doug. "Let me ask you something else. Could you show us—with your demonstration model—which way the earth is moving right now?"

"Well, let me look up some information," Julie said. She pulled out a little book and leafed through several pages. "Oh yes. It should be right about here, moving in this direction, away from the sun."

The jury murmured some more. It was true. The earth was moving *away* from the sun.

"Away from the sun," Doug repeated. "The exact words of Heather Hancock. As summer approaches, the earth is moving away from the sun. How odd."

"I object," Alison said.

"You should object, Ms. Krempel," Doug told her, "to the way Shep Sherman has tried to benefit from this impending doom."

Alison turned to Judge Stone. "Oh, please, Your Honor, Mr. Savage is making a mockery of science."

"So?" Doug said. "I can if I want to."

"He's distorting the facts," Alison protested.

"They were distorted when I got them," Doug replied stubbornly.

"Okay, order, order," Judge Stone almost shouted as she pounded her gavel. "That's enough. Why don't we take a break and let the jury absorb some of this information. Science Court is in recess."

6

FRED FEELS THE HEAT

"Okay, welcome back," said Judge Stone, calling Science Court to order after the recess. "Mr. Savage, are you finished?"

"Your Honor," Doug replied, "I haven't even scratched the surface." He stopped suddenly, frowned, and scratched his head. "Oh, wait a minute . . . scratch that. Yeah, I'm finished."

Then it was Alison Krempel's turn to question Julie. "Dr. Bean," she began, "earlier you said that because the earth's orbit is not a circle . . ."

"That's right," Julie confirmed. "It's slightly elliptical."

"Right," said Alison. "Now, because the earth's orbit is slightly elliptical and not like a circle, then sometimes the earth will be five million kilometers farther away from the sun than it will be at other times. Correct?"

"Correct," said Julie.

"So how much difference does five million kilometers actually make?" asked Alison.

"Asked and answered," Doug chimed in. Turning to Heather he added, "I've always wanted to say that."

"What does it mean?" Heather asked.

"I don't know," Doug replied. "But it's good lawyer talk."

"Overruled, Mr. Savage," Judge Stone declared. "I don't think we heard the complete answer the first time around."

"Yeah," Doug argued. "But Dr. Bean already said she couldn't walk five million kilometers."

"So?" asked Alison.

"So . . . it's a long way," came Doug's lame reply.

"Yes," said Julie, "but it doesn't make that much difference."

A murmur of astonishment rippled through the jury.

"What!" Doug exclaimed. "Five million kilometers doesn't make that much of a difference?"

"It's all relative," said Julie.

"Whose relative?" Doug demanded.

"I mean it depends on what we're talking about," Julie explained. "The earth is about one hundred fifty million kilometers away from the sun."

There was yet another murmur of astonishment from the jury.

"Wow," one juror said out loud.

"Is that far?" another asked.

"What's a kilometer?" yet another asked.

"That's almost ninety-three million miles," Julie explained. "You see, when we're talking about something that far away, another five million kilometers doesn't make a whole lot of difference."

"Mr. Savage," Alison broke in, "if you were driving to a place that you thought was one hundred fifty miles away, but when you got there you found that it was actually another five miles away, would you consider that a lot farther away?"

"Well . . . no," Doug admitted reluctantly.

"Okay, then," said Alison.

"Especially if I had a nice car," Doug added.

"Whatever." Alison turned back to the witness. "So, you were saying, Dr. Bean?"

"So the extra five million kilometers

really isn't enough to drastically change the climate on earth," said Julie.

Doug turned to Micaela, who was sitting right behind him. "Does she mean weather?" he asked.

"Not really," Micaela replied. "Climate is the average weather of a place over time."

"So what's weather?" Doug asked.

Micaela, correct as usual, explained to Doug that weather is the effect of the sun's heat on our atmosphere at a particular time. Doug asked Judge Stone if he could call Heather Hancock to the witness stand. With the judge's permission, Heather took the stand and Doug began his questioning.

"Heather, you went to Australia in June, is that correct?" he asked.

"Yes," said Heather.

"How was it?" Doug inquired.

"It was quite different but also very interesting," Heather replied.

"But you said it was cold," Doug argued.

"Well, I thought it would be a lot warmer than it was," Heather agreed. "The temperature hardly ever climbed above fifty degrees Fahrenheit."

"I didn't sneeze," said Fred.

"Neither did I," said Doug.

"Neither did I," said Shep.

"No, Fahrenheit." Heather was getting tired of the joke. "It was fifty degrees Fahrenheit. That's, uh . . . about ten degrees Celsius."

CELSIUS AND FAHRENHEIT ARE TWO DIFFERENT SCALES FOR MEASURING TEMPERATURE.

"Not very hot then, was it?" Doug asked.

"No," Heather replied.

"And what were the people in Australia saying about the weather?" asked Doug.

"They said it was winter," Heather responded.

"Winter in June," Doug sighed. "Has a sort of a sad ring to it, doesn't it? And that's when you did your investigation and found out that the earth was moving away from the sun, correct?"

"Yes," said Heather.

"No more questions," Doug concluded, convinced that he'd proven his point. "Your witness, Ms. Krempel."

"Thank you," said Alison. Then, turning to Tim, she asked, "Tim, are you ready?"

"Yep." Tim nodded excitedly. This was the moment he'd been waiting for—a chance to question a witness all by himself.

"Good luck," Alison said.

Trying to control his enthusiasm, Tim approached the witness. "Ms. Hancock," he began, "you said you did some investigating about this 'summer isn't coming' thing, right?"

"Yes, I read a book," answered Heather.

"A book?" Tim asked.

"Well, a couple of chapters."

"A couple of chapters?"

"Well, a few paragraphs."

"A few paragraphs?"

"Well, a sentence."

"A sentence?"

"Well, not a complete sentence, but a few words."

"A few words?"

"Well, not . . . yeah, just a few words," Heather admitted.

"You're right, Ms. Hancock," Tim remarked.

"I am?" Heather asked, surprised.

"You're right, Ms. Hancock," Tim repeated, "when you say you did a *little* investigating. No more questions, Your Honor."

"Good job, Tim," Alison praised him. Tim was all smiles.

"Your Honor," Alison continued, "if Mr. Savage is resting his case, I'd like to call a witness."

"Mr. Savage, are you resting?" Judge Stone asked.

"I'm wide awake," muttered Doug.

"I mean your case," said Judge Stone.

"Well, I don't know yet." Doug paused. "Am I going to lose?"

"He's resting his case," said Judge Stone. "Go ahead, Ms. Krempel."

"Thank you, Your Honor." And with that, Alison called Professor Parsons, another Science Court official expert, to the stand.

ORBIT EXPERT

Somehow, Professor Parsons had already taken the witness stand. "Ha, beat you to it," he said with a laugh. "I'm already here. Orbit expert, orbit expert, orbit expert. Are we still doing that? Ah, that's fun."

"Professor," Alison told him politely, "we're not doing that anymore."

"Oh, sorry," said Professor Parsons.

"Professor," Alison went on, "Mr. Savage seems to think that the earth moves closer to the sun in summer and farther away from the sun in winter."

"Mr. Savage," Professor Parsons replied, "the earth orbits, earth orbits, earth orbits—I got one in anyway—the earth orbits the sun . . ." He paused dramatically.

"Yes?" said Doug.

"The earth orbits the sun . . ." Professor Parsons continued.

"Yes?" said Alison.

"The earth—I'm enjoying this way too much," said the professor.

"Professor?" asked Judge Stone.

"Sorry," Professor Parsons apologized. "Just trying to have some fun since I lost out on that 'orbit expert' thing. Now, exactly where was I?"

"'The earth orbits the sun,'" members of the jury cried in unison.

"Wow, they're good," Professor Parsons commented. "How long have you been a jury? When you go to lunch, do all of you order the same thing? Okay, the earth orbits the sun on an angle." He produced the same model of the solar system that Dr. Julie Bean had used and held the earth in his hands. "May I use this demonstration model?" he politely asked.

"Sure," Julie replied. "But please don't wreck it."

"I won't," the professor promised her. "Wow." He started to sing, "I got the whole world in my hands . . ." Then he said, "People, you gotta have fun with science. Science is fun-o-rific. Ha-ha. Anyway, the earth is slightly tilted as it orbits the sun. Something like . . . this." He adjusted the earth to the proper angle.

"Objection, Your Honor," Doug said.

"What are you objecting to?" Alison demanded.

"Wouldn't you love to know," Doug replied with a smirk. "Your Honor, I'd like to take a brief recess while I talk to my client."

"Permission granted," declared Judge Stone. "We'll all take a little break. But before we do, I want to remind everyone to think about this earth orbit thing. Science Court is now in recess."

THE REASONS FOR SEASONS

After a short break, Stenographer Fred announced, "Science Court is now back in session."

"Okay," said Judge Stone. "We left off with Professor Parsons telling us that the earth is tilted."

"And then I said 'objection,' and then we took a recess. So, we're back to our break," Doug added helpfully.

"No, we're back to the case," Judge Stone corrected. "Ms. Krempel, continue, please."

"Thank you," said Alison. "Professor,

can you tell us how the tilt of the earth, and not the distance from the sun, causes the seasons?"

"Sure, I'd be delighted to," said Professor Parsons cheerfully. "You see, when the northern hemisphere . . ."

"Do you mean the top half of the earth?" asked Fred.

"Well, it's not really the top half, but okay," acknowledged Professor Parsons. "That's the northern hemisphere. When it tilts toward the sun, the rays are then more direct and hotter than rays that hit at an angle. The earth absorbs a lot of heat."

"What do you mean by 'rays that hit at an angle'?" asked Doug.

"Well," the professor went on, "these are rays that do not hit directly. When the hemisphere is tipped away from the sun, the rays hit the earth at an angle. The sun's rays do not hit the earth as directly, and we call these 'slanting rays.' The earth receives less heat, and the weather begins to get cold."

"Professor," said Doug, "I don't know how you do it, but once again you have somehow managed to baffle me."

Professor Parsons offered to demonstrate how slanting rays could be weaker than direct rays. Everyone seemed to agree that a demonstration would be a good idea.

"All righty then," said the professor. "Stenographer Fred, will you please hold this board at an angle in front of you while I spray water on it with this hose."

"Okay, but don't get me wet," said Fred.

"I know what I'm doing," the professor assured him. "Okay, ready, Freddy?"

"Ready, I think," Fred replied.

Professor Parsons sprayed the water from the hose directly at the board. Because the board was positioned at an angle, the water that hit the board splashed in several directions, causing the force of the water to be dispersed and reduced.

"That wasn't so hard," Fred said.

"That's right," Professor Parsons agreed, "mostly because the water dispersed at an angle, so it didn't have too much force. Now hold the board straight up and let me spray it again."

"Sure" Fred said cooperatively. "Hum, baby, hum it in here."

Professor Parsons sprayed the water again, but this time, the board was straight. The force of the water knocked Fred right off his chair.

"Hey, you knocked me down and got me all wet," cried Fred.

"Sorry, little fellow," Professor Parsons apologized. "Actually, I didn't spray the water any harder. I just hit the board more directly. That's why the spray felt more powerful."

"Just like the direct rays of the sun feel more powerful than the slanted rays?" asked Alison.

"Correct," the professor replied. "These direct rays give us our summer when we are tilted toward the sun."

"Wait a minute, Mr. Professor Know-It-All," Doug interrupted.

"You can just call me Parsons. It's the same thing," the professor said modestly.

"How do you explain to us the cold temperature Heather Hancock experienced in Australia . . . in June"— Doug was almost yelling now—"when we tilt toward the sun?"

"Actually, I just explained it," Professor Parsons replied.

"Not to me," said Doug. "And I was standing right here."

"Okay." The professor sighed. "Remember 'tilt'?"

"Yeah . . ." said Doug cautiously.

"Let's try a basic demonstration here," Professor Parsons said. "Mr. Savage, pick up your pen and hold it at a slight angle. That's the earth. Your water glass will be the sun."

"Why is my pen angled?" Doug wanted to know.

"That's the tilt of the earth," answered the professor. "Now, you see how the tilt is leaning toward the glass?"

"You mean toward the sun?" Doug asked.

"That's right," the professor replied. "That's the northern hemisphere, and it's now experiencing . . . what?"

"Summer?" Doug guessed.

"Right," said the professor. "But what happens to the southern hemisphere, where Australia is located?"

"Uh . . . the southern hemisphere tips away from the sun and has winter?" Doug speculated.

"Right, very good," said the professor. "That's why your client was finding it cold in Australia. It was tipped away from the sun. Now, move the pen, or the earth, around the sun, but don't change the angle. Then tell me what happens."

Doug did as he'd been told. "Well," he said slowly, "the bottom, I mean the southern hemisphere, is tipped toward the sun."

"What does that mean?" the professor asked.

"It's summertime?" Doug guessed again.

"That's right," the professor concluded. "You did it."

"That wasn't so hard," Doug said.

"Well," Judge Stone broke in, "any more questions?"

"Nope," Doug replied. "I'm ready for my closing argument."

Alison Krempel was ready for closing arguments, too. After a brief argument about who would go first, Doug Savage began.

"Good people of the jury," Doug said, finally getting it right. "Maybe my client and I did learn a little bit about the seasons. But did you know that Shep Sherman doesn't even know the first thing about teaching synchronized swimming?"

"Yes, I do," Shep protested. "I swam in college. Judge Stone, would you care to join me?"

"Sure," said Judge Stone.

As it happened, there was a large inflatable pool sitting in the courtroom. Shep and Judge Stone took off their clothes, revealing the bathing suits they were wearing underneath.

Together they jumped into the pool and began to swim a beautiful water ballet.

"Hey, you're good," Shep remarked to Judge Stone.

"I do thirty laps every morning," Judge Stone replied proudly.

Halfheartedly, Doug tried to make it to the end of his closing speech. "Uh . . . well," he said, "Australia, what's up with that? And kangaroos, huh? What's that all about? Thank you. Oh, and Shep's guilty, good people."

Without missing a stroke, Judge Stone called from the pool, "Thanks for keeping it short, Mr. Savage. Go ahead, Ms. Krempel."

"Your Honor," Alison said. "Uh . . . your swimming is a little distracting."

"Oh, of course," said Judge Stone.

Shep and the judge climbed out of the pool and wrapped themselves up in warm terry cloth bathrobes. Judge Stone wound a towel several times loosely around her head.

She resumed her place at the bench, shook her head to clear the water from her ears, and said, "Go ahead, Ms. Krempel."

"Thank you. Ladies and gentlemen of the jury . . ." Alison began.

Doug whispered to Heather, "She forgot to call them 'good people.' That's a point for our side."

"As you can see," Alison continued, "my client is an excellent water ballet instructor. He's really looking forward to his classes this summer. And there *will* be a summer. Heather Hancock's claim of summer not coming was totally ill-founded. Although it did bring up some common misconceptions."

Alison summed up the reasons for seasons that had been brought out in the trial. She reminded the jury that summer and winter are not caused by the earth moving closer to or farther from the sun, but by the tilt of the earth's axis. When the northern hemisphere's tilt is toward the sun, it gets direct rays and experiences summer, while the southern hemisphere gets slanting rays and experiences winter. Then, by the time the earth has revolved halfway around the sun, the northern hemisphere is tipped away from the sun and experiences its winter, while the southern hemisphere experiences its summer.

"Okay, jury, that was wonderful. Now, go to it," said Judge Stone.

The members of the jury practically tore off their clothes. As it turned out, they all had bathing suits on underneath, too. They squealed with delight as they leaped into the pool.

"Yippee!"

"Cannonball!"

"Last one in is guilty!"

Judge Stone banged her gavel. "Order!

Order in the court!" she cried. "I don't mean go swimming. I mean go and deliberate. And come back with a verdict."

The disappointed jury climbed back out of the pool.

"Oh."

"Right."

"Deliberate."

"We can deliberate better when we're all wet."

"Go," said Judge Stone. "Science Court will be in recess until the jury comes back."

9

SWIMMERS AND WINNERS

Jen Betters took the opportunity to conduct a brief interview with Doug. "Mr. Savage," she said, "it seems like you really learned a lot today. Do you still think that summer isn't coming?"

"Jen," Doug replied, "the question isn't whether or not summer's coming, or whether or not the tilt of the earth causes the seasons, or whether or not the earth's orbit is a slightly elliptical one. The question is, uh, . . . what is the question?"

The jury members took their places, and

Judge Stone asked if they were ready to deliver their verdict.

"Yes, we certainly are, Your Honor," the foreperson replied. "We find the defendant, Shep Sherman, not guilty of running a scam."

Doug turned to Heather and said, "Remember when we pretended my pen was the earth? That was good."

The foreperson continued, "And we find that Doug Savage's claim that there isn't going to be a summer this year is complete gobbledygook."

Doug pointed to Heather. "It was her idea."

"Okay, jury," said Judge Stone.

"One more thing?" the foreperson asked.

"Of course," Judge Stone replied wearily. "What was I thinking?"

"We'd all like to sign up for Shep's water ballet classes."

"Fine. Help yourselves," answered Judge Stone. Then she banged her gavel for the very last time and said, "Science Court is adjourned. Last one in the pool is a rotten judge."

"Is this what they mean by a jury pool?" Fred asked.

Judge Stone leaped into the pool with all the jurors right behind. Doug stood by the side dabbling his toes in the water. He was wearing water wings and an inflatable float around his waist, but instead of the typical sea horse or duck head, it had a head with a face that resembled his own sticking up in front. Professor Parsons waddled up to the pool in mask, snorkel, and fins and plunged in like a scuba diver.

"Professor Parsons, how's the water?" Alison called.

"Wet," Professor Parsons said with a happy laugh.

Jen Betters, her microphone in hand, approached Heather Hancock and asked, "Heather Hancock, now do you believe summer's coming?"

"Yes, and I'm glad," Heather replied. "I think I'll take those synchronized swimming classes after all."

"Well, that's it from Science Court," Jen summed up. "Until next time."

Just then, TV viewers all across the land heard Professor Parsons in the background yelling, "Hey! Let's get Jen!"

"See ya!" Jen laughed. And with that she ended her broadcast and jumped into the pool.

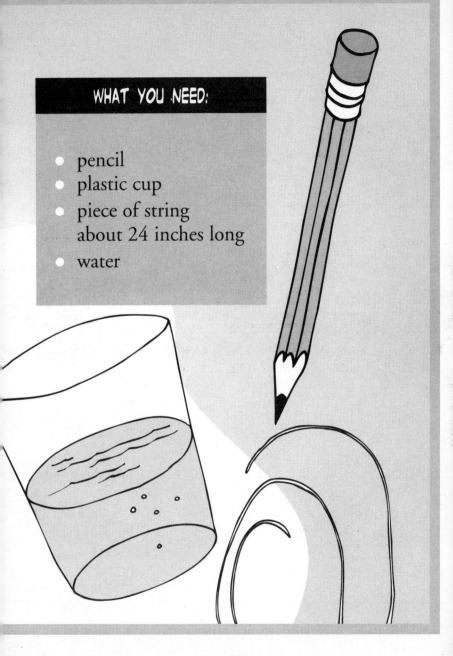

- pencil
- plastic cup
- piece of string
  about 24 inches long
- water

Using the pointed end of the pencil, punch two holes across from each other just below the top rim of the cup.

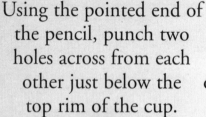

Thread the ends of the string through the holes in the cup and tie both ends.

Pour water into the cup until it is about one-quarter full.

Go outside with the water-filled cup.

5

While holding the string, swing the cup in a circle above your head. Start slowly, then spin the cup faster.

WHAT HAPPENS:

The cup flips onto its side as it spins around, but no water spills out of the cup.

WHAT IT PROVES:

The revolution of the earth around the sun, along with the earth's rotation on its own axis, produces a force called centrifugal force. The water in the cup moves outward because of centrifugal force, but the paper cup prevents it from flying away. In the same way, water on earth is prevented from flying out into space by the earth's gravitational force.